RABBIT'S PERFECT PARTY

by Ronald Kidd
illustrated by Vaccaro Associates, Inc.

Based on the Pooh stories by A.A. Milne [copyright the Pooh Properties Trust].

Edited by Ruth Lerner Perle
Produced by Graymont Enterprises, Inc.
Design and Art Direction by Michele Italiano-Perla
Pencil Layouts by Ennis McNulty
Painted by Lou Paleno

ISBN 0-7172-8445-X

Printed in the United States of America.

Grolier Books is a Division of Grolier Enterprises, Inc.

Rabbit was working in a sunny corner of the Hundred-Acre Wood. He moved through his garden, picking the last of his carrots. Then he stored them in his shed, with all the pointy ends facing one way and the roundy ends facing the other.

Another year's harvest was over. Everything had gone perfectly.

Smiling proudly, Rabbit went into his house and poured himself a glass of carrot juice. As he drank it, he looked at the calendar hanging over his kitchen table. On the last line, a day was circled in red.

Rabbit's birthday was only five days away.

SEPTEMBER

			1	2	3	4
5	6	7	8	9	10	11
12	13	14	15	16	17	12
19	20	21	22	23	2	25
26	27	28	29	30		

2

Rabbit thought back to some of his past birthdays.
One year, Pooh gave a party for him, with lots and lots
of food to eat. But all the food was honey. It was a good
party, but not a perfect party.

Another year, the party was at
Eeyore's house. There was hardly any
room inside, and the house was about to
collapse. It was a good party, but not a
perfect party.

4

Rabbit wished that just once he could have a birthday party that was perfect in every way. But who would give the party?

Rabbit thought and thought, and then he knew the answer. He, Rabbit, the cleverest animal in the Hundred-Acre Wood, would give his own perfect party.

Rabbit decided to keep it a secret because, for a party to be perfect, it had to be a surprise.

Rabbit pulled out his calendar and began to make plans. There were five days left before his birthday. Each day he would do a different job to get ready for the party. That way, when the big day arrived, all would be perfect.

That afternoon, Rabbit raked up the leaves in his yard. He had almost finished when Kanga and Roo dropped by.

Kanga said, "This isn't your raking day, is it?"

"Well, no," said Rabbit nervously. "I just thought the place needed tidying up."

8

Roo jumped into a pile of leaves shouting, "Let's play!"

"What a good idea," Kanga said to Rabbit. "You've been working too hard."

By the end of the day, Rabbit was exhausted—not from working, but from watching Roo scatter leaves all afternoon.

Now Rabbit had to rake leaves all over again so the yard would be perfectly clean.

The second day, Rabbit made decorations and planned the party games. He painted a neat banner that said HAPPY BIRTHDAY RABBIT. He was just finishing when Owl wandered by.

"Well, well, well," said Owl. "What have we here?"

13

Rabbit hid the banner behind his back. But the HA was still showing at one end, and the T was showing at the other.

"I know your secret," said Owl.

Rabbit's ears drooped. "You do?"

"Of course. You're making a sign that says hat, H-A-T. Which reminds me," said Owl, "did I ever tell you about the hat my great-uncle Timothy wore?"

For once Rabbit was happy to hear about Owl's great-uncle Timothy.

On the third day, Rabbit baked the perfect birthday cake. It was a carrot cake, of course. While it was in the oven, Pooh and Piglet came by to visit.

"Hello, Rabbit," said Pooh. "Piglet and I were just walking through the forest, and my nose told me to turn left at your house."

Piglet asked, "What's that you're baking?"

"Oh, nothing special," Rabbit answered quickly.

"The nothing special smells sweet," said Pooh. "I don't suppose it has honey in it?"

"Or haycorns?" said Piglet.

"No," Rabbit said. "It has carrots."

Pooh and Piglet looked at each other.

"I'm sorry, Rabbit," said Pooh, "but my nose just told me that we turned the wrong way. Would you excuse us?"

And off they went, leaving Rabbit with his perfect birthday cake.

17

On the fourth day, Rabbit was setting the table with his very best dishes when Tigger came bouncing along.

"Say," said Tigger. "Looks like you're throwing a party!"

"What makes you say that?" asked Rabbit.
"Those are your best dishes, aren't they?" Tigger said.
Rabbit looked at the dishes. "These? No,
they're just some old things."

Tigger said, "I love setting the table. That's what Tiggers do best!"

"Yes, I know." Rabbit gulped. "But sometimes certain Tiggers bounce so hard that they break the dishes."

"But if these dishes are old, then it doesn't matter, does it?" said Tigger.

20

"I'm not so sure about that," Rabbit said.

For the next hour, Tigger bounced around the yard tossing dishes on the table as he went. Rabbit was right with him, catching every single dish before it fell.

"Well, TTFN!" said Tigger when he finished. "Ta-ta for now!"

At last it was the day of the party. Rabbit brought out the decorations and games. Then he hung his birthday banner between two trees.

Finally he set the birthday cake on the table, among all his most beautiful dishes.

22

Rabbit stepped back to admire his work. At last, everyone would see what a perfect party looked like.

Rabbit stood at the table and waited for his friends to arrive. He waited and waited and waited.

But no one came.

What could possibly be wrong? Everything had gone perfectly. He had even managed to keep the party a secret, so it would be a surprise.

24

Rabbit sat up straight in his chair.
"Oh, no!" he cried. "I've done such
a good job of keeping the party a
secret that I forgot to invite anyone!"
Rabbit sat at his perfect
table, feeling like a very
unperfect Rabbit, and
singing sadly
to himself.

I'm perfectly neat and perfectly clean.
The cleverest rabbit that you've ever seen.
But here I am singing an unhappy song.
If I'm really so perfect—what's gone wrong?
My table is spotless, my dishes are swell,
My carrots are yummy 'cause I garden so well.
So how can it be that I'm feeling so bad?
I'm perfectly perfect … and perfectly sad.

Suddenly, Rabbit heard a hum. It floated out
of the forest, and behind it came Winnie the Pooh.
He was followed by Piglet, Owl, Eeyore, Tigger,
Kanga, and Roo.

28

"Hello, Rabbit," said Pooh. "We know you've been busy, but we just wanted to come by and wish you happy birthday."

"Oh, thank you," said Rabbit. "Thank you all."

Then Rabbit smiled and said, "I just happen to have a party waiting and you're all invited."

Everybody had a wonderful time. They ate and they talked. They giggled and played games all afternoon.

Some of the dishes broke, the cake fell over sideways, and the banner came down. But Rabbit didn't mind at all.

As long as his friends were there, it was a perfect party.

30